SWEDISH SAUNA

AN EROTIC ADVENTURE

VICTORIA RUSH

VOLUME 17

JADE'S EROTIC ADVENTURES - BOOK 17

COPYRIGHT

Everybody's an exhibitionist in disguise...

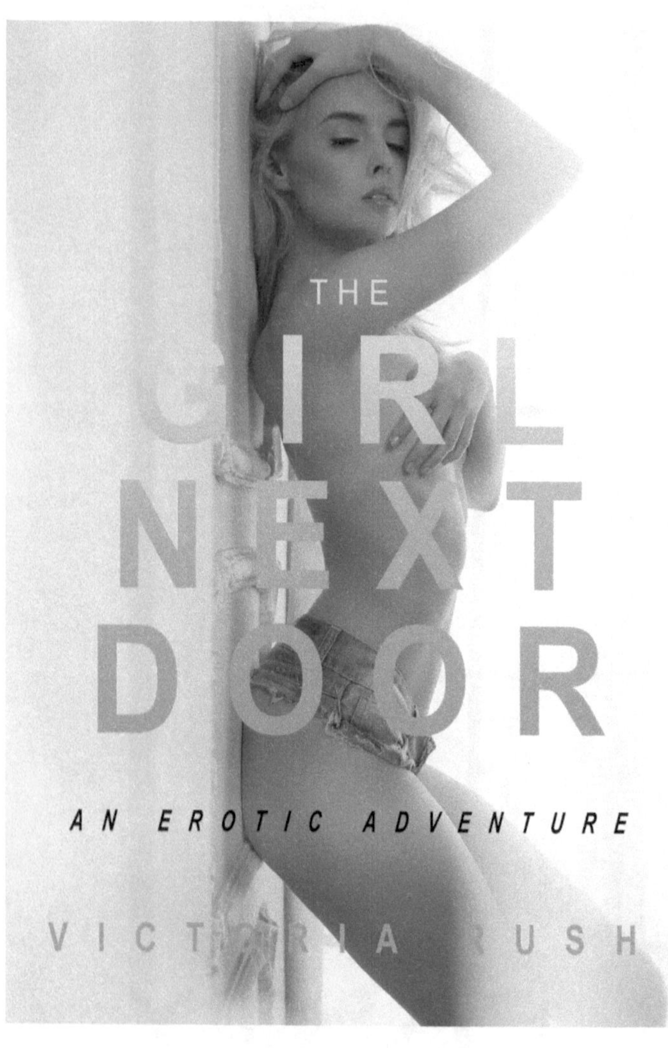

Spying on the neighbors just got a lot more interesting...

Everything's sexier in the dark...

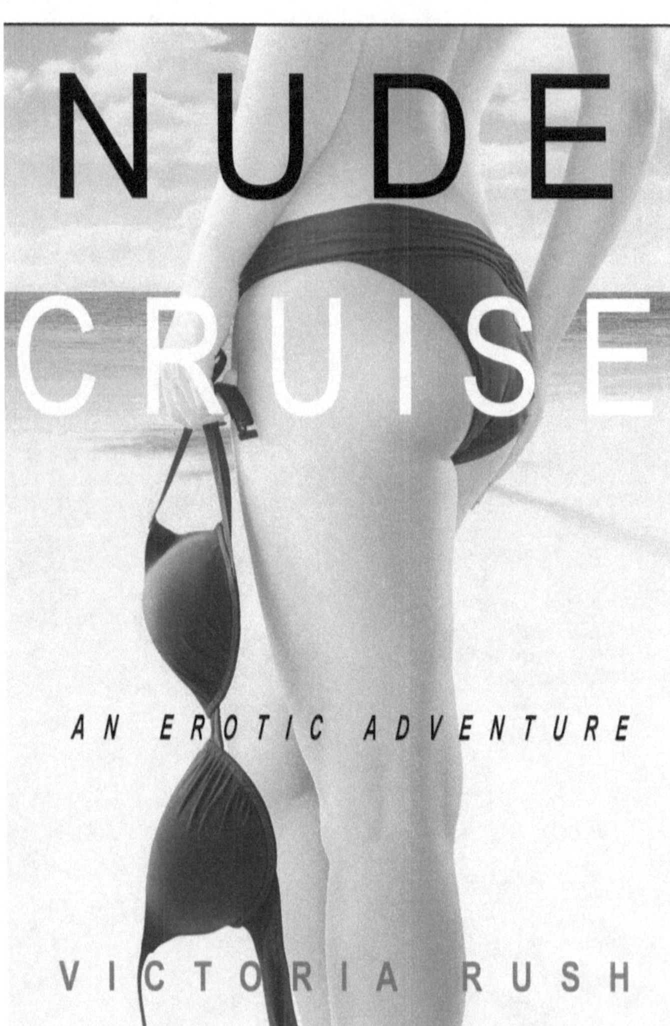

Some people get wet on a cruise for different reasons...

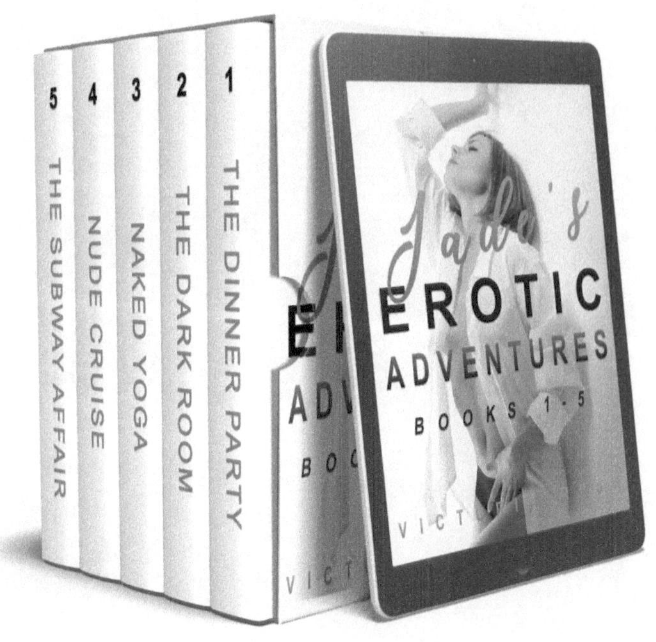

Books 1 -5 in the bestselling series - 60% off

For the uninhibited...

1

I knew this trip was going to be different as soon as I stepped onto the plane. The flight attendants aboard my SAS flight to Stockholm were drop-dead gorgeous. Not just typical cute-stewardesses pretty, like top supermodel stunning. Every one of them was tall, slim, and *built*. With high cheekbones, full pouty lips, and steel-blue eyes, I felt like was like I was being transported to another *planet*, not another country. One where everybody had natural blonde hair, sexy figures, and movie-star looks.

As I streamed down the aisle with the other passengers, I couldn't stop staring at the crew as they greeted the travelers with perfect smiles and lilting European accents. Instantly smitten, I felt my skin beginning to moisten while I gawked at them like a star-struck colt. When a hunky male attendant in a tight blue uniform offered to help me lift my overstuffed carry-on bag into the overhead storage compartment, I stuttered like an infatuated schoolgirl.

"Can I help you with that madam?" he offered.

"Um, yes," I said, flushing unconsciously. "I guess I overpacked for such a short trip."

As he effortlessly lifted my bag into the bin, I watched his pec muscles bulging under his neatly pressed shirt, with my face mere inches away from his chest.

"How long will you be staying in Sweden?" he asked, flashing me a full set of pearly whites.

With his handsome face and tall muscular build, he looked like a dead-ringer for the Scandinavian actor Alexander Skarsgard.

"Just a couple of weeks," I muttered.

"You can't be too careful at this time of the year," he said. "Wintertime in Sweden can be quite chilly and the nights are very long. It's best to bundle up."

"Thank you," I said, smiling at him warmly.

"Enjoy your stay," he nodded before moving down the aisle to assist another passenger.

When I plopped down into my seat, I suddenly became conscious of how wet my panties had become in the short time I'd been on the plane. A slightly older woman sitting across the aisle from me glanced at the beads of perspiration on my forehead and smiled.

"He had the same effect on me," she grinned. "Do you think *everyone* in Sweden is this beautiful?"

"I don't know," I said, shaking my head. "But if so, this should be one hell of an interesting trip."

I pulled out my phone and pretended to text someone on the screen. I knew it was going to be a long flight overseas, and I didn't want another Chatty-Cathy burning up my ear the entire way. I didn't want to lose another moment soaking up the dazzling flight attendants as they walked up and down the aisle.

When the doors finally closed and the jet began to pull away from the gate, I was happy to have an unobstructed view of the pretty stewardesses from my perch at the back of the forward cabin. As the lead flight attendant provided instructions over the intercom system, her pretty assistant took up position at the front of the aisle and smiled at me. Normally, I ignored these boring safety demonstrations, burying my head in a newspaper or playing games on my phone. But on this flight, virtually every passenger in the first-class compartment sat upright in rapt attention, with all eyes on the model at the front of the room.

While the attendant demonstrated how to properly use the seatbelts and oxygen masks, I squeezed my legs together to quell my throbbing pussy. Beyond her perfect bone structure and pretty updo under her tight bellman's cap, her skin was absolutely flawless. Her creamy alabaster tone radiated a natural blush over her Nordic cheekbones, her ramrod-straight posture reinforcing the impression of watching a model on the catwalk. When she raised her arms to point out the location of the emergency exits, her full breasts pressed against the front of her blouse, showing off her Amazon-perfect physique.

Jesus, I thought, listening to myself audibly panting as I watched her go through the motions. *No wonder men joke about the Swedish Bikini Team as their ultimate fantasy. These people really are as gorgeous as the legend says.*

As I sat in my chair getting more and more turned on watching the sexy flight attendant, I felt like I had a front-row seat at a Paris fashion show. I had the blind fortune of checking out some of the most beautiful people on Earth from in my own personal viewing room. Even my first-class leather chair made it seem like I was sitting in my home studio watching an Ingmar Bergman movie. I was glad the window seat next to me hadn't been filled, as I squirmed between the armrests trying to give my aching clit some much-needed stimulation.

But as I began to fantasize about taking the sexy flight attendant into one of the lavatories for a mile-high fling, the demonstration abruptly ended and she took a seat facing me at the front of the cabin in preparation for takeoff. Soon after, the jets began to roar and I felt the pull of gravity push me back against my seat as the plane lifted off the runway. When the attendant made eye contact with me momentarily, I fantasized that it was *her* pressing against me instead of the pull of the aircraft.

As she politely glanced around the cabin, I couldn't take my eyes off her. Whenever our eyes met, I looked away, embarrassed at my invasion of her personal space. As the heat between my legs began to build and the dampness in my panties spread, I peered up at the seatbelt sign, impatient to go to the restroom to relieve my pent-up tension. Watching this sexy goddess had gotten me thoroughly worked up and I knew it wouldn't take much to get me off. Even though it wouldn't be as glamorous as the usual in-flight fantasy, I'd have my own fun envisioning the two of us intertwined in the close confines of the tight water closet.

But when the bell chimed signaling that we'd reached cruising altitude and could remove our seatbelts, I found myself wanting to stay in my seat when I saw her getting up to begin the meal service. As she moved down the aisle offering a choice of beverages, I leered at her firm ass whenever she leaned over to hand a glass to one of the passengers. I was happy to be seated in the last row of the first-class cabin, with the relative privacy of the partition separating me from the coach compartment.

While I pretended to flip through the inflight magazine resting on my lap, my right hand began to inch between my legs in desperate need of stimulation for the aching nub underneath my jeans. The closer the cute attendant got to my seat, the more excited I got caressing myself under my magazine. By the time she reached my row, my eyes had already glazed over as I needed all my strength to contain the pleasure beginning to consume my body.

"Champagne?" she said, turning to me with a tray filled with tall goblets.

"Um, yes, thank you," I stammered, gripping the sides of my magazine tightly with two hands.

When she leaned over to hand me the glass, I couldn't help staring at her ample breasts spilling out over the top of her tight vest. A silver name tag dangled from her blouse reading Elsa.

"Can I get you anything else?" she said, smiling at me as I blushed shyly.

"What else are you offering?" I asked, my mind racing ahead with fantasies of her jumping into my lap while I ravished her in my quiet little alcove.

"Coffee, tea, juice," she offered. "Or would you prefer another cocktail?"

There was only *one* kind of tail I was thinking about at this particular moment.

"This will be fine for now, thank you Elsa," I said, biting my lip at the temptation to flirt with her further.

"I'll return in a little while with your meal service," she said. "Would you like the salmon or the filet mignon?"

I smiled, happy that I'd chosen to fly first-class for a change. Not only was the food and service a notch above normal, but I had a far better view of the pretty flight attendants in the smaller confines of the forward cabin.

"I'll have the salmon, thank you," I said, fixing my gaze on her brilliant blue eyes.

When she began walking back to the front of the plane, my eyes locked again on her firm ass.

That's not the only thing I'd like to eat right now, I thought, imagining my face buried between her thighs while she sat facing me on the sink in the lavatory.

While I continued undressing her with my eyes, my clit throbbed painfully under my tight jeans. After a few more minutes of anguished frustration, I finally stood up and bee-lined my way to the washroom. When I opened the door next to Elsa working in the galley, she turned around and glanced down at my midsection. I smiled at her, then closed the door and looked at myself in the mirror in shock.

Was she just checking me out? I thought. *What would be the chances of getting her to join me in here? Maybe if I leave the door slightly ajar...*

I shook my head, realizing the absurdity of my fantasy.

These kinds of things only happen in Penthouse Forum letters. There's no way a professional flight attendant would risk this kind of impropriety while on duty.

As I started unzipping my jeans to free my burning jewel, I noticed they were wet in the front. Peering down in the mirror, I saw that a large wet spot had formed in the crotch.

"*Fuck!*" I cursed out loud. "*That's* why she was looking at me that way."

I blushed in embarrassment at being found out, wondering how many other passengers had used this hiding place for release after watching these vixens go about their work. But at this point, the stain on the front of my pants was the last thing I was worried about. Right now, I just needed to get off, and quickly. I pulled off my jeans and underwear and hung them on the back of the door, then placed my right foot on top of the vanity. My slit stretched open as my flaming clit protruded out of its hood.

Gawd how I'd like to grind my pussy against Elsa's face right now, I thought.

I washed my hands under the sink then thrust two fingers deep into my pussy as I began to fuck myself, watching my reflection in the mirror.

If Elsa could only see me now, I dreamed. I had a pretty good figure for a thirty-six-year-old woman, and my looks were nothing to sneeze at either. Would she be able to resist keeping her hands off me, watching me fuck myself like this mere inches away?

As I began to feel the pleasure rising within me, I started to moan, pretending that Elsa was peering back at me in the mirror instead of my own reflection. I was happy for the background drone of the jet engines so that no one could hear me.

"Fuck me, Elsa," I panted. "Rub your beautiful body against me while we grind our pussies together and enjoy our own inflight entertainment."

While I imagined Elsa moaning in my ear and rubbing her tits against mine, my climax suddenly washed over me like a tidal wave as I grunted and spasmed over the sink. With my fingers embedded deeply in my hole, I jerked my hand up firmly against my mound while I gushed all over my palm. I was glad that I'd had the foresight to remove my jeans completely, because by the time I finished cumming, I'd produced quite a puddle on the floor underneath me.

Damn—I needed that, I panted, nodding at my reflection in the mirror.

I grabbed a few towelettes from the dispenser and wiped the floor, then washed my hands thoroughly and put my clothes back on. Realizing that I'd be revealing the stain on the front of my jeans for the entire cabin to see on my return trip to my seat, I loosened my blouse and draped it over the front of my crotch. Thankfully, it hung just low enough to cover the wet spot without looking too conspicuous. Then I brushed my hair and reapplied my lipstick to make myself presentable and opened the door. Elsa was still working in the galley, and she smiled at me as her eyes drifted down my body.

Had my ruffled blouse given away what I was up to in the lavatory? I wondered. *Or had she heard my moans over the noise of the jet engines?* At this point I hardly cared, and I smiled back at her with a flush in my cheeks as I walked back to my seat.

For the next hour or so, the cabin was fairly busy with the movement of the two first-class flight attendants serving and collecting the main meal service. I made small talk with Elsa whenever she passed by my seat, introducing myself and sharing my plans while I stayed in Sweden. When I told her that I intended to get in some snowboarding during my stay, she told me about the best resorts to visit in the northern part of the country. I was tempted to invite her to join me on my excursion, but my shyness got the better of me.

When things settled down after the meal service, she took a seat for a brief rest in one of the jump seats next to the main door. As she opened a magazine, I took the opportunity to study her body from head to toe. Her legs were crossed while she read the magazine, and the swelling of her calf resting on her knee amplified the sexy curviness of her long legs. I could see her dark leggings running up the underside of her skirt and wondered if they were full-height pantyhose or mid-thigh stockings with garters. It didn't take long for me to begin fantasizing once again about fucking her as she sat quietly reading her magazine.

Only this time I wanted freer access to my pussy, where I

could feel my slippery slit directly and rub my burning button without any impediments. I reached up and pressed the overhead call button, and Elsa looked up when she heard the chime. She peered down the aisle and noticing the light illuminated next to my console, she put down her magazine and walked toward me.

Damn, I thought to myself as I watched her glide down the aisle. *She even walks like a supermodel.* With her narrow foot placement down the cramped aisle, her hips swayed from side to side as her calves flexed with each step. I felt sorry disturbing her from her well-earned rest, but I needed one more thing from her.

"Yes, Jade," she said when she reached my seat. "What can I get you?"

"I was wondering if you had a blanket I could use to keep warm?" I said, peering up at her innocently. "It's a bit chilly in the cabin and I didn't bring a shawl in my carry-on bag."

"Yes, of course," she said. "I'll be back in a moment."

Elsa strolled back to the front of the cabin and opened a storage locker, pulling out plastic-covered packet. Then she walked back down the aisle and handed me the folded blanket.

"Was there anything else I can get to make your flight more comfortable?"

I paused for a moment raising an eyebrow, then shook my head.

"This should be fine for now," I said with a knowing smile. "I'm sure this will make the rest of my flight much more relaxing."

Little did she know what I *really* needed the blanket for. I just wanted some cover while I touched myself secretly in the privacy of my corner while I watched her from a distance.

"Just give me a ring if you need anything else," she said.

"I will, thank you Elsa."

As she began walking back up the aisle, I glanced at the woman sitting across the aisle from me and noticing that she had nodded off, I pulled my jeans and panties down below my knees. It felt exhilarating to feel the cool gust of the jet breeze rushing up between my bare thighs. When Elsa returned to her seat, I glanced up at her and smiled, then she picked up her magazine and lowered her head.

Perfect, I thought. *You lose yourself in your little distraction while I lose myself in you as I get distracted doing other things.*

I snaked my right hand under the blanket and moistened the tips of my fingers with my slippery juices, then pulled them up and began circling my throbbing gland. Watching Elsa's pretty face while she read her magazine was the perfect aphrodisiac while I enjoyed myself under my blanket. As I rubbed my hard nub, I looked at her lips covered in clear gloss, imagining what it would feel like to have them surrounding my pearl. It didn't take long for me to start squirming in my seat as the pleasurable feelings began spreading throughout my body. Elsa peered up over the top of her magazine, and I looked away in embarrassment realizing she'd caught me staring at her once again. But when I glanced back at her, I noticed that she was still looking in my direction as she darted her eyes between my face and the bump in the blanket between my legs.

Did she sense what I was doing? I wondered. *Had I been too obvious in my amateur subterfuge?*

Either way, there was no way I was going to stop, because I'd gotten far too worked up to abandon my solo entertainment. As I returned her gaze, I slowly resumed rubbing my clit under the covering. At first, I did it in such a way that she'd have a hard time recognizing any suspicious movement. The last thing I needed was to get arrested for lewd or inappropriate behavior. I knew airlines had a low tolerance for disruptive passengers, and I had nightmares of being carted off the airplane in handcuffs in front of my fellow passengers upon landing.

But far from ignoring me or raising the alarm to her colleagues, Elsa seemed just as interested in what I was doing as I was in her. While she shifted her eyes between the magazine and the other passengers to distract attention from her watching me, I became bolder and bolder in my actions. I spread my legs wider apart and began to move my hand more quickly over my mound.

When it became obvious to Elsa what I was doing under my blanket, she lifted her leg and swung her thigh on top of her other knee. This time, I could see the curvature of her exposed thigh as her skirt hiked half way up her leg. While my hand began to move more forcefully under my blanket, I saw the muscles in Elsa's legs flexing rhythmically as she squeezed her legs together on her chair.

Is she stimulating herself while she watches me get off? I wondered.

Her quiet act of self-pleasure ratcheted up the intensity of my feelings even more, as I moved my other hand under the blanket and began to play with my sopping slit while I rubbed my bean with my other hand. Seeing that I was getting more worked up watching her at the front of the cabin seemed to increase Elsa's courage in lock-step, as the flexing action of her legs increased in speed and intensity. Recognizing that she was stimulating herself in full view of the rest of the cabin was an insane turn-on for me, and I thrust my fingers deep into my snatch, pummeling myself as I watched the flush on Elsa's face begin to spread down her neck onto the top of her chest.

I was aching for release, and when I saw her suddenly hunch over and pretend to cough as her body began to spasm, I gushed all over my hand, cumming hard for the second time during the flight. When she sat back up and glanced in my direction, I was still jerking in my seat with my mouth agape. She tried not to stare at me to avoid drawing attention from the other passengers, but she couldn't help flitting her eyes back toward me until I finally collapsed in my seat in delirious exhaustion.

For the rest of the flight, the two of us pretended like nothing had happened, continuing to carry on casual conversation while she attended to the needs of rest of the passengers. When we began to descend into Arlanda airport, I pulled myself together and collected my belongings in preparation for deplaning.

But by now, the stain in the front of my jeans had spread to the size of a grapefruit from the puddle I'd been sitting on, and I waited for the rest of the first-class passengers to disembark before rising from my seat. Holding my purse strategically over the front of my pants to hide the wet spot, I collected my bag from the overhead bin then made my way to the front exit door. Elsa was standing beside the exit wishing everyone well, and I paused for a moment before heading out onto the jetway.

"Thank you for such a memorable flight," I said, taking her hand and clasping it warmly between mine. "That was the most exceptional customer service I've ever experienced."

"The pleasure was all mine," Elsa smiled, placing her other hand over top of mine. "Enjoy your stay in our lovely country. Perhaps I'll see you on the return leg of your journey."

"I'll look forward to that," I said, realizing that I was

holding up the rest of the passengers from exiting the plane. "Bye for now."

As our hands began to separate, Elsa pressed her fingers into the palm of my hand and I felt a strip of paper fall into my palm. I looked at her inquisitively, and she simply smiled and nodded. The moment I got through the jet bridge into the relative privacy of the main terminal, I stopped and unfolded the strip of paper she'd handed me.

Hope you enjoyed your inflight experience, the message read. *Drop me a line when you get settled in Stockholm. Perhaps we can enjoy a few more rides together on the slopes of the interior. Elsaflygirl@gmail.com*

I smiled a silly grin as I pulled my carry-on bag toward the exit door.

That wasn't the *only* kind of riding I had in mind for the remainder of my trip.

2

After I checked into my hotel room, I started up my laptop and opened a new email message. As my hands hovered over the keyboard, I pondered how best to respond to Elsa's invitation. Had she been thinking the same thing I was when she mentioned taking a few more 'rides' together? Was her choice of the words 'slopes of the interior' code for getting undressed and touching each other's naked bodies? Or was she just referring to snowboarding on the mountains of the north country?

Fuck it, I thought as I began to tap the keys. Either way, I wanted to see more of her—any way I could. We'd already shared an undeniably erotic moment together. There'd be plenty of other opportunities to get to know each other better during a few days of snowboarding together.

Hi Elsa, I typed.

Thank you for your lovely note. It was a pleasure meeting you on my flight to Stockholm, even if it was quicker than I hoped. I'd love to have a chance to get to know you better. Do you have some free time to do some snowboarding before your next

*flight? I'll be in Sweden for a week and I've got an open itinerary.
Let me know if you'd like to get together,*

   Best wishes,

   Jade.

For a few moments, I sat in front of my computer hoping she'd reply right away to my message. But after a few minutes, I realized how foolish it was of me to expect her to pause her normal routine just because we'd shared a passing moment on the transatlantic flight. I wondered how many *other* passengers had been equally obsessed by her and made similar passes. Surely, she'd have her choice of the most successful and prettiest travelers if she really wanted to strike up a more serious relationship.

I slammed my laptop shut and got up to distract myself from my single-minded infatuation. After all, I'd come to Sweden for a lot more reasons than just to meet new people. Between exploring the fjords, seeing the northern lights, and shopping the old city of Stockholm, there was plenty to do during my one-week stay. I'd even thought about staying one night at the famous ice hotel in Jukkasjarvi. But mostly I just wanted to recharge my batteries from my boring life in Chicago. I'd been flitting from one shallow relationship to another and needed a change. I figured the further I got away from home, the easier it would be for me to forget about my troubles. I hadn't planned on being gobsmacked by the most beautiful woman I'd seen in a long time.

After I unpacked my clothes and arranged my toiletries, I couldn't help checking my computer for new messages. To my surprise, I had a letter from Elsa marked only a few minutes after I'd sent my note. As I clicked to open the message, my stomach fluttered in excitement wondering what new adventures awaited me.

Jade, her message began.

How nice to hear from you so soon after our flight. I've been thinking of you too, and was wondering if you'd like to join me and a few friends for a little ski trip. My parents have a cabin near the resort town of Are, and I'm traveling there tomorrow with a couple of girls from the airline for a few days of R&R. The easiest way to get there is by train from the central station in Stockholm. There's a departure around 9 p.m. tonight that will get you in to the village early in the morning. If it's not too quick a turnaround for you, I can pick you up when you arrive and we'll all head out to the hill together. You're welcome to stay with us at my parents' place until you're scheduled to leave.

Looking forward to more adventures together,

Elsa

While I read the message, I could feel my heart beating in my chest as I imagined spending more time with the pretty stewardess. But now I'd have to share her with her friends, and I wondered if that would get in the way of our having some more intimate moments together. But she'd already demonstrated that she was attracted to women, and it didn't take long for me to imagine the bunch of us enjoying some quality après-ski time in the cosy confines of her alpine cabin. Besides, if the *girls* she was referring to were the other attendants on the flight from Chicago, the more the merrier. I'd have my very own fantasy bikini team to play with for a few days.

I quickly accepted her invitation, then packed up my things and checked out of the hotel, grabbing a cab to the downtown train station. I was surprised how packed it was for a Saturday evening, and after purchasing my ticket to Are, it took a while to get my bearings and find my way to the right departure track. When the train pulled up, I was impressed at how sleek and clean it looked. So far, I'd found everything about this country to be beautiful, polished, and efficient. Even my round-trip fare for the six-hundred-kilo-meter trip was thrifty, costing less than a hundred bucks.

When I stepped inside the train, I placed my snowboard gear and travel bag in the overhead rack then settled into a seat next to the window. Everything about the train was first-class, from the spotless upholstery and gleaming handrails to the crystal-clear panoramic windows. Even the *people* on the train looked stylish, dressed in fashionable parkas and fur-lined hats.

When the train began to exit the station, I peered outside the window and watched the passing streetscape flash by. I marveled at the pretty architecture of the multi-colored townhomes and plentiful canals running through the city. Within thirty minutes, the train was hurtling through the snowy forest of the interior, and I soon nodded off with my head resting against the glass.

Three hours later, I woke to the feeling of the chilly window pressing against my head, and I looked outside to see a strange glow moving in the night sky. Realizing this was the fabled northern lights I'd read so much about, I craned my neck to take in the eerie spectacle. The luminous bands swirled and morphed into ever-changing shapes and patterns, like a giant fluorescent ghost dancing in the sky. Now I understood why the indigenous people of the arctic gave such spiritual meaning to this supernatural light show. The swaying bands of color almost looked like a living organism, undulating in perpetual rhythm in the northern atmosphere.

There's another thing I can knock off my bucket list, I thought, staring up at the sky with my eyes agape in wonder.

But as the train continued north, the skies began to fill with clouds, and I checked my watch to see what time it was. The nights were over sixteen hours long at this latitude at this time of year, and I didn't want to arrive at my final destination unprepared. Even though it was approaching 8 a.m., it was still pitch-black outside and the train would be arriving into Åre within thirty minutes. I went into the onboard lavatory to check my makeup and have a quick pee, then wrapped a scarf around my neck under my snow jacket, wondering if I'd prepared sufficiently for the cold Nordic weather.

When the train stopped, I gathered up my gear and headed for the station exit. Elsa hadn't been very specific about how we'd find one another at the train station, so when I got outside I stood on top of the steps surveying the parking area. There were a lot of passengers milling about with cars pulling up into the pick-up zone, so I pulled off my woolen cap and began waving in the general area of the logjam.

A few seconds later I heard a car horn beeping and a late-model Volvo SUV pulled up in front of me with the headlights flashing. The passenger window rolled down and a familiar face smiled at me, motioning for me to approach the car. The rear latch swung open and Elsa stepped out of the driver's seat waving back at me. I smiled at her and threw my board over my shoulder as I walked in their direction. When I got to the car, she gave me a big hug and threw my gear in the rear compartment on top of a bunch of other boots and snowboards.

"Did you have any trouble finding your way here?" she asked.

"No," I smiled. "It was pretty uneventful, other than the spectacular pyrotechnics in the evening sky."

"Ah yes," she said. "The aurora borealis. Was that the first time you'd seen the northern lights?"

"Yes—and it was even more beautiful than I imagined."

"We'll have lots more opportunities to view it over the next couple of nights from my cabin."

She opened the rear driver's side door and motioned me inside.

"But first, let's have a bit of fun on the slopes. I think you'll find the *daytime* views can be almost as pretty in this part of the country."

When I stepped inside the vehicle, two familiar-looking blonde girls turned toward me and smiled. I recognized both of them instantly as the other flight attendants on my inbound trip, and dressed in their pastel snowboard outfits they looked even prettier close-up.

"Do you remember Astrid and Inga from the flight?" Elsa said.

"Of course," I said, thinking I'd died and gone to heaven, surrounded by the three gorgeous women. "How could I forget?"

On the way from the station to the ski resort, we made small talk about my plans while in Sweden and what my life was like back in Chicago. The girls said they traveled there frequently, and I immediately returned the invitation, inviting them to stay with me the next time they were in town. But the whole conversation was a blur as I kept flitting my eyes between the three striking Vikings sitting next to me in the car.

When we got to the ski hill, we all carried our gear up to the lodge then went inside for a quick breakfast and coffee. The girls ordered cereal composed of muesli, fermented milk, and strawberries, and I followed along, trying to sample the local cuisine. It wasn't as bad as it sounded, and I soon gobbled down the crunchy yogurt-tasting concoction on my empty stomach. Then we wolfed down some strong coffee and went downstairs to the locker room to change into our snowboard gear. The three girls all seemed quite adapt at getting into their heavy boots, and when they pulled their goggles over their toques in preparation to exit the cabin a couple of minutes ahead of me, I shook my head in wonderment.

"You girls look like you've done this a few times before," I said, gazing up at their pretty two-piece parkas.

Elsa smiled, kneeling down to help me lace up my boots.

"There's not a lot to do during long winters here in the hinterland," she said. "It's pretty much a choice between hockey or snow skiing. And the airline frowns upon our taking part in contact sports. Something about keeping ourselves in top condition for our guests."

"I can see why," I said, peering at the Swedish beauties. "I wouldn't want to mess with perfection either if I had your looks."

"You know," Elsa said, holding a hand out to help me off the bench. "With your fair skin and light hair, you could easily pass for a Swede too. And I think you're selling yourself short. You're just as pretty as any Scandinavian girl. Speaking of, let's get out there while we still have good light. The rides close in a few hours and it looks like we've had some good powder overnight."

When we got outside, the girls snapped on their boards then shuffled their hips forward as they began to glide to the base of the nearest lift. When we neared the front of the line, we positioned ourselves four abreast and sat down on the wide chair as it swung around to pick us up. As it picked up momentum and lifted us off the ground, my pussy pulsed in excitement feeling the hips of the other girls pressing up against my sides.

"So what brings you to Sweden?" Astrid asked, puffing a cloud of condensed air into the chilly breeze as she spoke.

"Besides the beautiful people and the gorgeous scenery?" I said, peering out over the mountainous landscape. "I guess I was just looking for something new. I was getting kind of bored with my usual routine in Chicago. It's been a while since I've been on a trip outside the country."

"Well if you're looking for something different," Inga said, smiling at the other girls. "Stick with us. We'll be happy to introduce you to some of our more interesting Swedish customs. The après-ski scene can be just as much fun as the daytime opportunities."

Elsa noticed my hands gripping the safety bar in front of me tightly as I shivered under my light snowboard ensemble.

"Are you warm enough?" she said, placing her mittens over mine on the bar. "I noticed you weren't wearing as many layers as the rest of us under that thin parka."

"I'm used to dressing for the mild midwestern winters back home. I guess I wasn't quite ready for the temperatures up here."

"You'll warm up once we get out on the slopes," she said. "All you need is a little exercise to get the blood flowing."

She peered forward as our chair neared the top of the mountain.

"What kind of trails do you like to take? How experienced a snowboarder are you?"

"I don't get out as often as I'd like," I said, glancing down the steep slope underneath our lift. "I used to be pretty decent when I was younger, but it's been a couple of years since I've hit the slopes. Maybe something intermediate to start?"

"No problem," Elsa said. "Just head to the left when we get off the lift. We can start out on the blue trail. It's wide and gently sloping, with lots of room for us to carve wide unobstructed turns."

When the chair reached the crest of the hill, we all pushed off while I struggled to stay balanced as it thrust me forward. The other girls seemed far more composed and confident, shifting their weight expertly backwards as they dug their edges into the soft corn while I wobbled unsteadily, trying to keep my board from getting away from me.

"Ready?" Elsa said, flashing me a brilliant smile.

"I think so," I hesitated.

Seconds later, the girls pointed their boards down the hill and began carving up the light powder in tight serpentine patterns, three abreast. I watched them for a few moments, marveling at how effortless they made it seem, but also how pretty their tight asses looked twisting and swaying as they kicked up light sprays of powder, schussing their way down the meandering slope. Not wanting to get left too far behind, I shifted my weight forward and tentatively pointed my board on a diagonal line across the slope.

At first, I was reluctant to commit myself fully into the fall line, but as I began to shift my weight forward and back on my board, I was pleasantly surprised by how easy I could turn in the freshly fallen snow. Before long, I was carving figure eight patterns overtop the trails left by the other girls and smiling with a giant grin as I began to find my groove. About halfway down the hill, I noticed the they'd pulled up on a flat section of the slope and I skidded to a halt a few feet in front of them.

"*Damn*, Jade," Elsa said as I huffed a stream of fog into the cold air, trying to recover my breath. "You know how to *ride*, girl. That's some pretty sweet carving you were doing down the trail. We're going to have to step up our game to keep up with you."

"Hardly," I smiled. "You're the ones making it look easy. I'm already starting to feel the burn in my legs. You might need to give me a couple of days to ease into this, or else I might need a wheelchair to get back onto the plane for the ride back. Something tells me you guys have had a bit more practice at this than me."

"Maybe," Elsa said. "But you sure aren't any slouch. Why don't you go first this time and we'll follow. Show us your best Lindsey Vonn moves."

I thought it ironic that they'd likened me to the pretty American downhill champion who'd recently turned the European circuit on its ear.

"I'm not *that* good," I said. "I'll just be happy if I can make it down the rest of the way without wiping out."

This time I flipped my board forward and headed straight down the fall line, rapidly picking up speed as I arched my body from side to side, reveling in the soft champagne powder of the Swedish resort. When I got to the bottom of the hill and stopped at the base of the lift, the three other girls followed close behind and skidded to a stop beside me.

"It looks like you've found your legs," Elsa said. "You can carve, girl. I was admiring your form all the way down."

"Are you referring to my ski technique or my skimpy little outfit?" I smiled.

"Both. I had a hard time staying on the course with such a pretty distraction in front of me."

"Glad I was able to keep you distracted," I smiled. "I'm hoping there'll be lots of other opportunities to divert your attention over the next couple of days."

The four of us spent the next couple of hours carving

the hills, taking increasingly steep and exciting trails before we decided we need a rest. When we stopped near the bottom of one of the trails, Elsa looked over toward me and smiled in a heavy plume of mist.

"Are you ready for some fika?" she said.

Not knowing exactly what that was, but sounding pretty close to fucking, I nodded eagerly, happy to have a different kind of alonetime with the girls.

"Let's head into the lodge," Elsa said. "I don't know about you guys, but I could eat a moose after a hard morning of riding."

"Count me in," Astrid said.

"I could use a warm cup of coffee right about now," Inga nodded.

"Is that what fika is?" I said, pinching my eyebrows in disappointment.

"Yes," Elsa said. "In Sweden, coffeetime is more of a social gathering opportunity than just an excuse to get charged up on caffeine. Let's go inside and rest up for a bit while we get warmed up. We don't want to turn your body into rubber on the first day."

We trudged into the lodge and found an open spot next to a large wood-burning fireplace. As the girls began to take off their heavy parkas and outerwear, I couldn't stop scanning their shapely figures in their tight, form-fitting sweaters. The cute reindeer motifs reminded me of Pippi Longstocking, but their swelling breasts and hourglass figures reminded me more of that other Swedish meme. There was something about the warmth of the roaring fire and the sweat dripping down the back of my neck from the exertion on the slopes that was quickly getting me worked up. As I continued undressing the girls with my eyes, my mind began to wander to the possible après-ski activities that Elsa had mentioned.

"Shall we get a bite to eat?" she said, catching me eyeing up her body.

"Absolutely," I said, trying to quell my churning insides. My stomach wasn't the *only* body part that needed attention right now. I needed a distraction quickly before I peeled off their clothes right then and there and jumped their bodies in my mind's imagination.

As we strolled up to the food line, I once again followed the girls' lead. Everybody was ordering hot pea soup or oven-cooked pancakes with ligonberry jam and maple syrup. But when it came time to order coffee, they all looked at me with a strange expression when I ordered a latte with extra cream and sugar.

"What?" I said, looking at the girls with a puzzled expression. "You guys are looking at me like I just ordered *antifreeze*."

"We don't put all that extra stuff in our coffee in Sweden," Elsa said. "We like to take it straight-up, where we can enjoy its natural goodness."

"Mmm, I get that," I said, glancing at her shapely ass in her tight leggings. "Straight up it is."

When we returned to our table next to the fire, I was surprised how good the pancakes and soup tasted. I was so used to the typical American brunch of bacon and eggs that I'd almost forgotten about the pleasures of a foreign diet. Even the plain coffee tasted unusually good, as I savored the natural flavor of the north African bean.

While we made small talk about our favorite trails at the resort, I couldn't help staring at the girls' shapely figures in their tight sweaters as their chests expanded and contracted while they ate their food. The orange flames from the fireplace cast a warm glow on their faces, accenting their natural beauty. By the time we'd finished our meal, my entire body was burning and flushed in excitement.

"So what do you guys do for fun after playing on the hills all day?" I said, hoping to plant the seeds for some more adventurous après-ski activities.

Elsa looked at her friends for a moment then peered at me with a devilish grin.

"Have you ever participated in a polar bear plunge?" she asked.

"Isn't that where people jump into freezing cold water in the middle of winter?" I said, shaking my head in bewilderment. "Isn't that kind of painful and dangerous?"

"Not the way we do it. We only stay in for a short time then head into the sauna to warm up. It's actually quite refreshing. After a hard day of snowboarding, the cold water actually reduces muscle inflammation and speeds up your recovery time."

"Do you guys wear some kind of special insulation?" I said, not quite buying Elsa's dubious explanation.

"Actually, the best way to do it is in the nude. The less clothing, the better. You don't want any cold clothing clinging to you when you get out of the water. We'll have terrycloth robes ready for you to warm up quickly. But the best part about it is the sauna afterward. Feeling the warm steam all over your newly cleansed skin is absolutely heavenly. It's is a tradition we Swedes have been practicing for centuries."

The idea of seeing the three pretty flight attendants in the buff quickly eliminated my concerns about the discomfort of the procedure. It actually sounded like a lot of fun, and my mind was already racing ahead to all the possibilities once we got in the sauna.

"When in Sweden..." I smiled, cocking my head playfully. "You guys certainly aren't holding back giving me the full immersion experience. I'm eager to learn *all* about your special customs."

"Good," Elsa said, reaching down to lace up her boots. "Let's get back out on the slopes while we've still got some good light. It'll turn dark in a couple of hours and we haven't even tried the most challenging trails."

I smiled nervously, feeling the burn in my thighs when I stood to zip up my jacket.

Hopefully the *rest* of my body will still be able to function by the time these girls are ready to stop torturing me, I thought.

3

———

By three o'clock, the shadows were beginning to lengthen over the mountain, and the four of us headed back into the lodge to collect our belongings. I was actually looking forward to the dip in the cold water to help relieve my aching muscles. As we drove through the dense forest on the way to Elsa's cabin, I marveled at the natural beauty of the Scandinavian landscape. Heavy pillows of snow hung over the roofs of quaint chalets nestled among the tall evergreen trees, like icing on gingerbread houses. The woods got thicker and thicker, until we emerged onto a clearing with a small wooden cabin at the edge of an ice-covered lake.

"Here we are," Elsa said, pulling her car up next to a broad porch at the front of the structure. The setting reminded me of a prototypical arctic winter scene, like something out of a Christmas fairy tale.

"Let's go inside and get the fireplace going," she said. "You'll need to get warmed up before taking a dip in the lake."

When we stepped through the front door, I was

surprised how cold the cabin was as I rubbed my hands over my shoulders trying to increase the circulation.

"Sorry about the chilly temperature," Elsa said. "We normally keep the furnace set just high enough to keep the pipes from freezing." She nodded toward a giant stone fireplace with tall stacks of wood framing the opening. "We prefer to heat our houses the natural way. There's nothing like the sound and smell of freshly cut birch cackling in the open hearth."

She kneeled down in front of the fireplace and rolled some newspaper into little balls then placed some kindling over top of them and struck a match. The material quickly burst into flame, and as she stacked the silver logs over the iron grate, the fire soon began roaring, throwing pretty sparks against the safety screen.

"*That's* what I'm talking about," I said, taking a seat on the mantle next to the fire, rubbing my cold fingers together.

"Can I get you something to drink while you warm up?" Elsa said. "Maybe a hot chocolate or a black coffee?"

"If it's not against the rules trying something a little sweet," I smiled. "A hot chocolate would be lovely."

Elsa disappeared into the kitchen and reemerged a few minutes later with a platter holding four steaming cups. She handed one to each of us, then the girls sat down on heavy armchairs facing me. I could feel my cheeks begin to flush as I gazed at them with the orange glow from the fire dancing over their pretty faces.

"So what do you think of our country so far?" Elsa said.

"It's a little chillier than I imagined," I said, clasping my mug between my palms to warm up my still-tingling hands. "But everything about it certainly is beautiful."

"We'll get you warmed up soon enough," she smiled. "Would you like a little tour of my chalet? We've got the place all to ourselves for the next few days, and you'll need to know where to find the water closet and other amenities. Besides, I need to stoke the coals in the sauna to heat it up in preparation for our polar bear plunge."

"Oh yeah," I said, huddling closer to the fire. "I'd almost forgotten about that."

As I followed Elsa through the different rooms of the cabin, I was struck by how small the place was. With only two bedrooms and one washroom, I wondered how four girls would comfortably share the space for more than a few days. But I hesitated asking about the sleeping arrangements, hoping we'd be able to at least double-up in the small space. I was already beginning to plan how I'd nestle up against Elsa on the pretense of getting warm as a prelude to more intimate exploration.

When we reached the back of the cabin, Elsa opened a heavy door and the smoky scent of fresh cedar filled my nostrils as I peered into a large wood-paneled room. Every surface of the interior was lined in reddish-brown planks of wood, with wraparound wooden benches on two levels surrounding a small metal stove topped with gray rocks.

"Wow," I said, inhaling the smoky scent. "This room is even bigger than the bedrooms. You must spend a lot of time in here."

"Having a daily sauna is like a spiritual experience for us Swedes," Elsa nodded. "It's part of our DNA. There's no better way to relax and wind down after a busy day."

She stepped toward the little stove and placed a large ladle into a wooden bucket of water. As she spilled the liquid gently over the glowing rocks, a hot steam began to fill the room with a pleasant eucalyptus aroma.

"That's an interesting way to warm up a room," I said, my

heart racing at the thought of soon lying in the heavenly space next to the three beauties.

"Radiant heat is the cleanest type of heat," Elsa nodded. "Plus, the humidity does wonders for cleaning out your lungs and your pores. You'll feel like a new woman after spending a couple of hours in here."

"I can imagine," I said, beginning to feel my pussy perspire at the thought.

"Are you ready for a bracing swim first?" Elsa said, flashing me a sly grin.

"I guess so," I murmured, preferring to stay in the comfortable and aromatic environment of the steam room.

"Let's get changed out of our outerwear," she said, opening an adjacent closet. "I've got some heavy robes to keep you warm before and after the swim."

We all returned to the living room, where the three girls began to disrobe. I hesitated at first, nervous to reveal my naked body among a group of strangers. But as they peeled off their layers showing more and more skin, I slowly began to undress. Their firm breasts bounced on their chests as they pulled off their undershirts and I couldn't help gasping when they finally removed all their clothes. All three of them had creamy pale skin and Playmate-perfect figures. With nary a hair to be found anywhere on their bodies below their flowing blonde locks, my pussy pulsed in excitement as I stared at them unashamedly.

"Jesus," I said, shaking my head in amazement. "Is *everybody* in Sweden in this good shape? You guys all look like somebody straight out of a beer commercial."

"Yeah—we get that Swedish Bikini Team thing all the time," Elsa said, shaking her head. "I'm not sure Budweiser did us any favors creating that image of Scandinavian girls for North American consumption."

She gave my body a quick going over as I pulled off the last of my underclothes.

"But you're no slouch either, Jade. With your blonde locks and athletic figure, you could pass for a Swedish girl any day."

I stood awkwardly facing the three girls, feeling the heat of the nearby fire burning the back my naked body.

"I'm just happy to be mentioned in the same *sentence* with you guys, let alone be thought of as one of your countrymen," I said, hoping to deflect everyone's attention from my naked figure. "Are we going to do this or what?"

"Of course," Elsa said, handing out terrycloth robes and slippers to each of us. "But be careful as you walk down the path toward the water. There's plenty of ice, and the rocks are quite slippery. You might want to hold my hand as you make your way over the flagstones."

We all put on our gowns, then Elsa opened the front door as I felt a rush of cold air enter the cabin.

"Come on, scaredy-cat," she said, holding out her arm for me. "We don't want to let the cabin get cold again. Let's take a dip before you lose your nerve."

I wrinkled my forehead, then took Elsa's hand as the four of us scampered down the frozen flagstone path to a small dock extending out over the water. When we got to the end of pier, I noticed a ten-foot-diameter hole cut into the ice covering of the pond and I looked at Elsa with an incredulous expression.

"You want me to go in *there*?" I said with my eyes agape.

"Just for a few moments," she said. "I promise you'll enjoy it. There's nothing so invigorating as a brief plunge into freezing-cold water to charge up your adrenaline. Are you ready?"

"I don't know..." I said, pulling back on Elsa's hand.

Suddenly, Astrid and Inga threw off their robes and jumped into the black pool, emerging from the frigid surface hollering in delight.

"Come on in, Jade," Inga said, flinging her wet hair behind her head. "The water's lovely. Come experience the crystal-clear water of our natural habitat."

"Natural habitat?" I scoffed. "Maybe for a *polar bear*."

Elsa turned to face me and squeezed my hand.

"Come on Jade, you're just torturing yourself standing out here in the cold air. We'll jump in together and it'll be over before you know it. Then we can all get nice and cozy in the warm sauna."

There was something about the way she said *nice and cozy* that encouraged me to get this over with.

"Ready?" she said, dropping her robe onto the dock.

I looked at her sexy body shining in the bright moonlight and pulled off my frock.

"One–two–THREE!" she shouted, then she leaped off the dock pulling me into the pitch-black lake.

It took a moment to register the feeling of the cold water surrounding my body as my mind was still in shock at the audacity of what we were doing. But within seconds, I could feel the painful burn of the freezing depths as my teeth began to clatter while I treaded water.

"Isn't it *fabulous*?" Elsa said, smiling at me with a big toothy grin.

"Ye-yes," I stuttered, trying to block out the numb feeling rapidly spreading over my body. "That's one thing you could call it."

"Look, up at the sky," she said, peering upward. "The northern lights are even more beautiful this far away from the city."

"It's stunning," I said, recognizing the swirling green

clouds. "But I think I could appreciate it better dressed up in a warm sweater from your front porch with a warm cup of coffee resting on my lap."

"Okay," Elsa nodded. "I think we've exposed you long enough to the natural elements for one night. Let's get out of here and warmed up."

She swam to the front of the dock and climbed up a small wooden ladder then held out her hand to me as she bent down over the edge.

"Give me your hand so you don't slip getting up."

As I kicked my way to the ladder and placed my hands on the rungs, I could feel my muscles shaking as I tried to pull myself up. Elsa grabbed one of my hands and lurched me out of the water, then wrapped one of the robes around my shivering body. As she held me close trying to share her body heat, I watched the other two girls emerge from the pool with beads of water running over their sexy figures. Their areolas contracted with deep goose bumps as their hard nipples extended out from their breasts almost a full inch. For a moment, I forgot that I was standing near-naked in subfreezing temperatures soaking wet while I admired their sexy bodies.

"Come on," Elsa said. "Let's get back into the cabin and warm up in the sauna. I think you're ready for a new kind of Swedish experience."

The four of us scurried up the path, then Elsa opened the front door and we scampered over the hardwood floor into the sauna. While Elsa poured three ladles of water over the steaming coals, the room soon filled with the soothing sensation of the humid heat. I sat down next to the stove, with the other three girls sitting on the two levels directly opposite me.

"There," Elsa purred. "Doesn't that feel a little better?"

"Yes," I said. "But not enough to take off my clothes quite yet. I'm still warming up in this nice cozy robe."

"Feel free to keep it on for a little longer," Elsa said. "But we normally like to take our saunas in the nude. Soon you'll begin to sweat and you'll want to give your pores a chance to open up and let your body cleanse yourself."

As if on cue, Astrid and Inga unfastened their belts and pulled their robes open, revealing their glistening breasts.

"Yes," I panted. "I want to experience *everything* here in Sweden the same way you native girls do."

"You know," Elsa smiled. "I kind of like watching you covered up. It reminds me of our little affair on the plane."

"Oh?" I said. "You remember that still?"

"How could I forget?" Elsa grinned. "That was the most interesting flight I've had in a long time."

"You seemed to be enjoying yourself almost as much as I was."

"I have a little secret to confess," she said. "I had a little help of my own while I watched you."

"Really?" I said, pinching my eyebrows together in confusion. "I saw you flexing your thighs, but–"

"There was a little more than that going on. I had something *inside* while I was rubbing myself."

"Inside?"

"Ben-wa balls. Have you ever tried those before?"

"I've heard of them but never tried it. How do they work?"

"You gently rock your hips or squeeze your legs together, and they roll around inside your pussy providing a very erotic sensation. It's quite an exquisite feeling. I have them inside me right now."

"*You do?*" I said, widening my eyes in surprise. "How do you keep them from falling out?"

"It's not hard to keep them in using your Kegel muscles. In fact, it's considered a good way to exercise those muscles to maintain optimal sexual function."

Elsa paused for a moment, as she began to spread her legs apart.

"Can you do me a favor and play with yourself under your robe while I replay our little erotic encounter on the plane?"

"*Hell* yes," I said, happy to see that Elsa and the other girls were just as interested as I was moving our relationship to the next level of intimacy.

As I slipped my hand under my robe, I felt my still cold and clammy skin over the front of my hairless mound. But as I moved my fingers over my slit, I felt my warm natural juices beginning to lubricate my vulva.

"Mmm," I purred, watching Astrid and Inga spread their legs further apart as they watched me. "I *like* seeing you in your natural habitat."

"Yes," Elsa groaned, rocking her hips gently on the wooden bench. "You're very pretty, Jade. I've been dreaming about watching you up close ever since our flight ended."

"I was so happy when I read your note," I smiled. "I've pleasured myself many times replaying that moment over and over."

"As have I," Elsa said, rubbing her thighs together as she opened her robe wider for me to see her juggling tits. "And I wasn't the *only* one who enjoyed that memory," she said motioning to the other girls sitting on the bench beside her.

Astrid and Inga nodded as they moved their hands between their legs and began to circle their nubs.

"You *told* them?" I said, feigning surprise.

"Of course. We share everything together. You're not the

only one who likes a little play time between girls every now and then."

I smiled at the revelation that they were all bisexual like me.

"It looks like the only person missing from your troop is the hot flight attendant who reminds me of Tarzan," I said

"You mean *Erik*?" Elsa said. "He's quite a dish to be sure, but I think he prefers to bat for the other team as much as we do."

"You mean he's gay?" I said. "What a shame. I was undressing him on the plane almost as much as I was you girls."

"Not to worry," Elsa smiled. "I'm pretty sure between the three of us that we'll be able to keep you properly entertained during your stay."

"I hope so," I panted, watching Astrid and Inga place their fingers inside their pussies while they jilled themselves watching me play with myself.

"Open your robe now," Elsa ordered. "Let me see exactly what you were doing under that blanket on the plane. I want to watch your pretty body while you pleasure yourself. It's just us girls this time and nobody else is watching."

I didn't need any more encouragement as I began to feel the pleasurable sensations spreading throughout my body. The rising steam from the coal stove had increased the room temperature to well over one hundred degrees and I didn't need any more excuses to fully disrobe. I took my gown off my shoulders and threw it on the bench beside me and spread my legs wide apart to let the girls see my glistening lips.

"Yes," Elsa said. "Show us what you were doing with your fingers under that blanket."

By now, I was burning up inside from the rising passion

as I watched the three goddesses touching themselves while they watched me. I plunged my middle two fingers into my snatch and pulled my palm against my throbbing button, stroking myself with increasing intensity as the three women writhed on the wooded benches in front of me. Elsa spread her legs further apart, rocking her hips forward and back while she rubbed her clit in tight little circles.

"Yes, Jade," she purred. "Fuck that sweet pussy with your pretty fingers. I want to watch your body heaving and shaking again when you come."

"Damn, Elsa," I said, feeling the wall of pleasure rapidly building inside my body. "This is a feast for my eyes. I'm going to come soon."

"Yes, my pretty American," she said. "Let us watch you satisfy yourself while we pleasure our bodies. I'm close too."

As I watched the three beauties rocking their bodies on the warm planks, I felt my body fall over the precipice as I clamped down over my fingers, hunching over in a series of rhythmic spasms. With the pressure built up inside my pussy from my fingers damming the flow of my juices, I pulled my fingers out of my hole and began spraying long streams of fluid over the steaming wooden floor. Seeing me squirting my juices while racked in pleasure soon pushed the other girls over the edge, and within seconds all four of us were shaking and groaning in the steamy fog of the sauna.

"Now I see why you were covering yourself up when you left the plane," Elsa sighed when she came down from her climax. "That's one part of the experience I definitely missed. You are one talented and sexy lady, Jade."

"Not nearly as sexy as the three of you," I said, catching my breath. "That was the hottest show I've seen in a long time."

"I have to agree," Elsa smiled, peering at her colleagues. "What do you think girls? Is this the sexiest passenger we've ever had on our transatlantic flight?"

"Definitely," Astrid nodded. "I've seen a lot of fuckable passengers in my day, but nobody I've wanted to get down and dirty with as much as this one."

"And we're just getting started," Elsa grinned. "There's so many other ways we can have fun together now that we're free of all the limitations on the plane. What's your ultimate fantasy, Jade? What would you like to do now that you have the three of us all to yourself?"

"Oh my God," I said, realizing all my dreams were about to come true. "My mind is racing with so many possibilities right now. But honestly, I'd just like to watch you three do your thing together. This is the like the ultimate erotic video, watching three gorgeous girls touching each other. I'll be happy to get in on the action soon enough. For now, let me just soak up your fabulous figures a little longer while I watch you get a little more interactive."

Elsa smiled as she peered over at Astrid and Inga.

"What do you say, girls? Shall we indulge our guest in her little fantasy?"

"I thought she'd never ask," Inga smiled, shifting her body closer to Elsa.

"If you're just going to *watch*," Elsa said, pinching a little string between her legs and pulling two glistening chrome balls out of her slit. "Would you like to try my little toy? I think you might find it makes for a more engaging experience."

"Absolutely," I said, raising my eyebrows as I peered at the intriguing balls.

Elsa stood up and walked across the floor then handed

me the slippery orbs. I could smell the musk of her scent on the globes and I looked up at her, grinning a broad smile.

"Just be sure to leave some of the string hanging out your opening," she said. "They can get pretty far up inside you in the heat of the moment and you don't want to lose them up there. Once you place them inside, you'll find plenty of ways to stimulate yourself. Enjoy."

Elsa returned to the other side of the room, sitting on the upper bunk while Astrid stood on the lower bench facing her with her back toward me. As she lowered her face toward Elsa's pussy, Inga sat between her legs and tilted her head up as Astrid planted her mound over her chin. Within seconds, all three girls were rolling their hips in a three-way ménage as they began to grunt and moan in unison.

Watching them pleasuring themselves just a few feet in front of me soon got my juices flowing again as I awkwardly pressed the two chrome balls into my slit. They slipped inside easier than I imagined, but it felt unusual to have such a strangely shaped object inside me other than the usual dildos and vibrators I was accustomed to.

But as I began to rock my hips slowly on the bench, I could feel them sliding forward and back against the walls of my pussy, and I soon began to mew and groan along with the other girls. It didn't take long for me to get comfortable with the pleasurable feeling of the slippery balls stroking the walls of my pussy, and when I placed my fingers against my dripping clit, I felt a jolt of electricity running through me.

This is a little different, I thought. *Why haven't I tried this before?*

Now I understood why Elsa brought them with her wherever she flew. With their unobtrusive form factor and concealed placement, no one would be any the wiser as she went about her duties receiving gentle, sensuous stimulation whenever she moved.

As I watched Elsa spread her legs wide apart and Astrid humping Inga's face while they ate each other out, I began to rock my hips faster and faster watching the girls bucking and moaning in front of me. With Inga's legs splayed far apart as she rubbed her bald pussy with her glistening fingers, and seeing the base of her chin planted firmly against Astrid's mound, watching the three girls fucking themselves in the superheated environment of the aromatic sauna was the most erotic thing I'd seen in a long time.

When Elsa placed her hands beside Astrid's head and pulled her face harder against her pussy as she locked eyes on me, I suddenly felt a surge of pleasure engulfing me. With our mouths yawning wider and wider apart in shared ecstasy, I couldn't hold back any longer.

"Oh *fuckkk*," I groaned in pleasure, my body beginning to shake once again in another intense orgasm. I could feel the Ben-wa balls rolling around inside as my pussy walls contracting rhythmically against them, sending me into new paroxysms of pleasure.

Watching me shaking uncontrollably on the steamy wooden planks seemed to bring Elsa to a new level of pleasure, and soon she also began jerking spasmodically as she held Astrid's face tightly against her pussy. Like a chain reaction, Astrid suddenly became weak at the knees as she slumped forward against Inga's chin with her buttocks shaking like a bowl of water. Feeling Astrid coming all over her face, Inga raised her hips off the bench and began flapping her thighs in and out in mutual ecstasy. Realizing that all three girls were coming together took me to another level, and within seconds I was having my third powerful orgasm of the afternoon.

After we all come down from our climaxes, I suddenly became aware of the ache in my quads from my hard day of snowboarding. I'd been so lost in the moment watching the other girls having fun and pleasuring myself that I'd forgotten I'd just had the most intense exercise in months.

I'll have to take it easier on the slopes tomorrow, I thought, *if I'm going to keep up with these girls and enjoy some more off-piste action.* The après-ski experience had been even more exciting and adventurous than the vigorous snowboarding exercise. I wanted to save myself for the next step in my Swedish immersion.

4

Over the course of the next few days, Elsa, Inga, Astrid and I made love many more times between our snowboarding, polar plunge, and sauna escapades. By the end of the week, I'd experienced every erotic entanglement with the three girls that I'd fantasized about on my initial flight to Sweden. When it finally came time to say our goodbyes, I was sad to leave but thrilled to have had the opportunity to spend so much quality time with the three Scandinavian beauties.

As the four of us drove back to Stockholm in preparation for my return flight to Chicago, we talked about reconnecting stateside, but I never expected to see the girls again. We'd had our moment of glory together, and that was enough for me. I'd cherish the experience forever and carry enough memories to keep me entertained for quite some time into the future.

But I still had one last flight with the girls, and I planned to make the best of it. Elsa and I had talked over the last couple of days about how we might be able to arrange a *real* mile-high liaison, and my body was tingling all over in anticipation of the trip. After I passed through airport security and collected my boarding pass, I smiled at Elsa and Astrid as I boarded the plane and took my seat near the back of the first-class cabin. The same woman I'd met on my inbound flight was sitting across the aisle from me again, and I smiled politely before pretending to check my email messages.

While the rest of the passengers shuffled onto the plane, I tried to keep myself distracted reading a magazine while I squirmed uncomfortably in my seat. Watching Elsa do the safety demonstration drove me crazy knowing she was receiving internal stimulation the whole time from her Ben-wa balls. I cursed myself for not remembering to buy some of my own to keep me entertained during the long flight.

But when the demonstration was over and the girls took their seats in preparation for take-off, Elsa winked at me, giving me a sly smile. Within thirty minutes, we reached cruising altitude and Astrid and Elsa began delivering the meal service. It was difficult restraining myself from interacting with the girls in a more familiar manner, but I continued playing the role of naive first-time traveler to maintain their professional demeanor. Besides, I knew that very soon we'd be able to dispense with the charade and have one last chance at resuming our special relationship.

When the meal service was over, Elsa and Astrid seemed more generous than usual offering the passengers their choice of alcoholic beverage. Before long, most of the early-morning travelers had nodded off in their seats from the combined effects of full stomachs and the alcohol-induced sedative. The girls took their seats at the front of the cabin for a brief rest, and after briefly scanning the attentiveness of the passengers, Elsa nodded toward me and tilted her head in the direction of the forward lavatory.

I carefully glanced around the cabin and when I saw that everybody was either sleeping or absorbed in their reading material, I rose from my seat and slowly made my way up the aisle. As I opened the door to the lavatory, I smiled at the two flight attendants and they winked back at me. When I closed the door behind me, my heart began racing a million miles an hour thinking about what we were about to do. Whether it was from the danger of being exposed or from the excitement of soon reconnecting with my Swedish lovers, I wasn't sure. But either way, my panties were already soaked from the rush.

It seemed to take forever for Elsa to join me in the lavatory, and after a few minutes I began to wonder if some of the passengers had woken up or requested additional aid. Not knowing what to do with myself, I began to disrobe and hung my clothes on the peg over the door. Looking at my fully naked body in the mirror, I began to play with myself imagining her touching me in the private cubicle. Just as I was about to come remembering the sight of the three sexy stewardesses in the sauna, suddenly the door swung open and Elsa stepped inside. She looked at me hunched over the sink with my hands between my legs and smiled as she shut the door quietly behind her.

"It looks like you've gotten started without me," she said. "That's my girl. We won't have too much time to do this while Astrid is keeping watch."

She stepped toward me then reached up to the paper towel dispenser above the sink and laid a protective layer of towels over the vanity.

"Get up on the sink and spread your legs for me," she instructed. "I need to fuck you right now. I've been dreaming about this ever since I saw you."

"That makes *two* of us," I sighed, turning around to face

her while I lifted myself up onto the sink, splaying my knees against my naked breasts.

Elsa took one look at my glistening pussy and hiked up her skirt, revealing her bald pussy framed between black garter stockings.

"I *knew* you were naked under there," I smiled, feeling my juices beginning to run over my perineum all the way down to my throbbing rosebud.

"Would I have it any other way?" she said, pressing her mound against mine as she locked lips with me and pressed my back against the cold glass mirror.

"Mmm," I hummed, feeling her wetness touching mine. "Fuck me, Elsa. I've been waiting for this a long time."

Elsa lifted her knee and extended her right leg, placing her foot against the mirror beside me. Her legs were separated like a pair of open scissors, with our pussies grinding together as we moaned in each other's mouths. For a moment, my mind reeled at the audacity of what we were doing, but it didn't take long for me to begin feeling the rising tide of pleasure spreading throughout my body. Elsa had already revealed her incredible flexibility to me in our prior erotic encounters, but this new technique with her fucking me in a perfect split took me to a whole new level of sexual intensity.

"*Oh God,*" I panted as I listened to our wet labia smacking together while we ground our pussies against one another. "Are you still carrying those love balls inside you?"

"You tell *me,*" Elsa grunted as I felt her buttock muscles contract against my sweaty palms.

Suddenly, I felt the slippery balls pass out of her pussy into mine as her pussy began contracting in the initial stages of orgasm.

"Come with me, Jade," she panted. "I want to feel you spray all over me like you did in the sauna."

"*Fuck* yes," I hissed, feeling my climax suddenly overtake me from the feeling of Elsa's balls swirling around inside me. "I'm cumming, Elsa!" I groaned. "I'm cumming so hard!"

As my walls contracted tightly over the steel balls and I began squirting all over Elsa's pussy, the balls suddenly spurt back out as we grunted in unison from the feeling of the slippery orbs rubbing between our slits. We tried to remain as quiet as I could in the narrow confines of the lavatory, but it was difficult to stifle our screams of mutual ecstasy as we ground our hips together on the shaking vanity.

When the two of us came down from our powerful climaxes, I peered down, noticing that I'd soaked Elsa's black stockings with my juices.

"Sorry, sweetie," I said, shaking my head. "But I couldn't help myself. When you passed me the balls, I had the hardest climax I've had in a long time."

"Not to worry, babe," Elsa smiled, reaching into her purse beside the counter. "We flight attendants come prepared for every emergency."

As she began to pull out a new pair of stockings, we heard a tap on the door. Fearing we'd be caught by a passenger wanting to use the lavatory, my heart began thumping wildly as my eyes widened in fright. Elsa held a finger to her lips then tapped back twice on our side of the door, and the person on the other side tapped back quickly three times in succession. She smiled back at me then opened the door as Astrid squeezed in next to us.

"*What the...*?" I said, pinching my eyebrows in surprise. "Who'll be our lookout in case another passenger needs to use the washroom?"

"Everybody's completely passed out and sleeping peace-fully," Astrid said. "We've got a few more minutes to have a little fun. I couldn't resist. Listening to you guys has gotten me all worked up."

"We were *that* obvious?" I asked.

"Only if you were standing next to the door. The sound of the jet engines drowned out most of the noise."

"Okay," Elsa said. "But we'll have to act fast. Let's let Jade take the driver's seat this time. I'll listen for any passenger pings next to the door."

Astrid hiked up her skirt and leaned back against the sink, pulling me toward her, rubbing her mound against my slippery pubis.

"Who's wearing the balls *this* time?" she smiled, peering toward Elsa.

Elsa passed Astrid the glistening balls and she slipped them inside her pussy, then she pulled me closer and began kissing me hard on the lips. Although we were standing in an upright missionary position this time, we were able to angle our hips just enough to touch our clits as we ground our pussies together. As I began to feel my pleasure rapidly escalating, thinking our little tryst couldn't possibly get any more erotic, suddenly Elsa stepped behind me and thrust her fingers into my snatch as she began finger-fucking me from behind.

"*Yes, Jade!*" Astrid panted, feeling Elsa rocking our hips together. "I want to feel you cream all over me when you cum. Fuck me with your pretty American pussy."

Feeling Astrid's pussy grinding against mine with Elsa finger-fucking me from behind as she squeezed my tits was a sensory overload. Within seconds, I began climaxing once again as I squirted a stream of powerful jets inside Astrid's hole while we moaned into each other's mouths, gripping each other tightly. Elsa pressed her own mound hard against my quivering buttocks as the three of us groaned in simultaneous ecstasy with the cabin full of passengers just outside the door seeming a million miles away.

When we all recovered from our climaxes and realized what a mess we'd made, the girls quickly changed stockings while I cleaned up the room. When we finally collected ourselves and prepared to leave, Elsa placed her ear to the door and nodded.

"I'll go first to make sure the way is clear," she said. "If everything looks good, I'll tap twice then you can both come out."

Astrid and I nodded, then Elsa opened the door and closed it quickly behind us. Within a few seconds, we heard a soft double-tap and the two of us exited the washroom as I made my way back to my seat past the still-sleeping passengers. But when I got to my chair, I peered over at the woman sitting next to me and she opened one eyelid, smiling at me.

Fuck, I thought. *We've been made.*

But seeing that she wasn't overly perturbed by the incident, I settled back into my seat, feeling the dampness of Astrid's and Elsa's juices clinging to my pussy pressing up against my moist panties. I glanced toward the front of the cabin and saw the girls sitting quietly beside one another in their jump seats with a sexy glow still on their cheeks. I smiled at them and mouthed the words *Thank You*, blowing each of them a kiss.

Seconds later, the woman sitting next to me pressed her call button and when Astrid walked down the aisle to attend to her, she asked for a blanket. When Astrid returned with the cover, the woman placed it over her lap and moments later I noticed her hand slip underneath it as she began to stroke herself between her legs. Sitting in the middle row of seats, she wasn't able to make direct eye contact with Astrid or Elsa, so she turned her head and smiled at me. As I saw her eyes begin to glaze over in self pleasure, I smiled back at her with our shared secret.

It looked like I wasn't going to be the *only* one enjoying a little mile-high thrill on our trip back from Sweden.

Everybody's an exhibitionist in disguise...

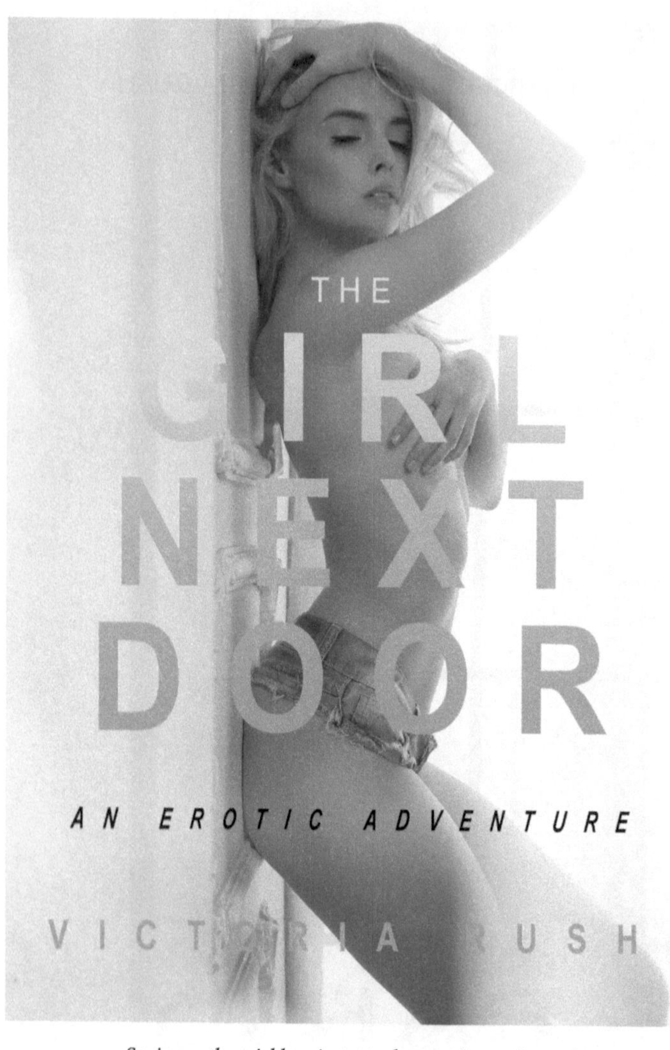

Spying on the neighbors just got a lot more interesting...

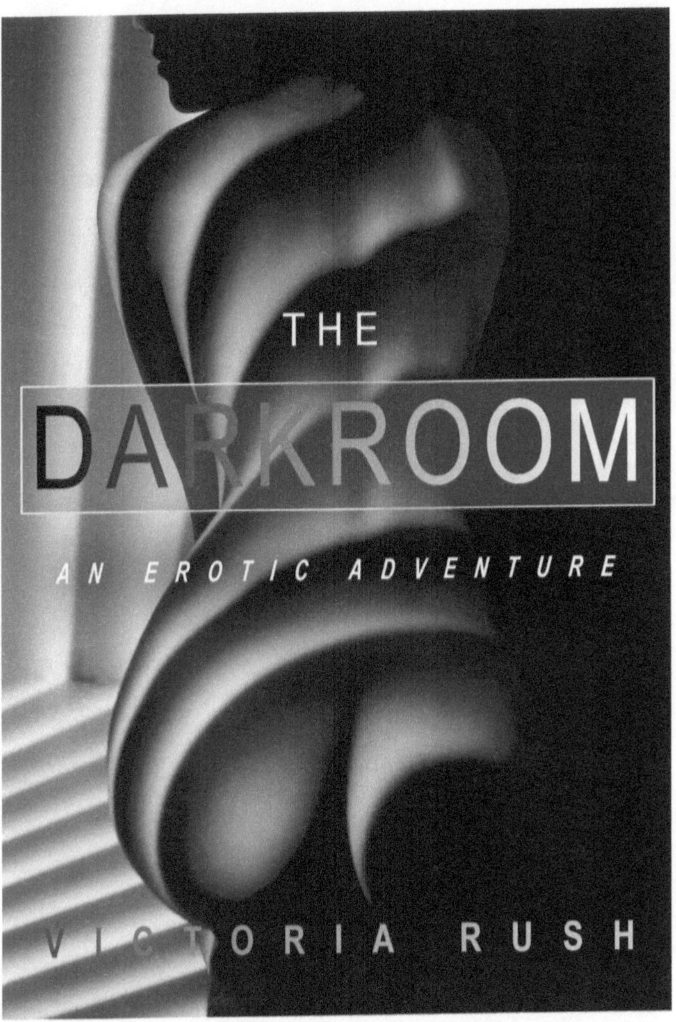

Everything's sexier in the dark...

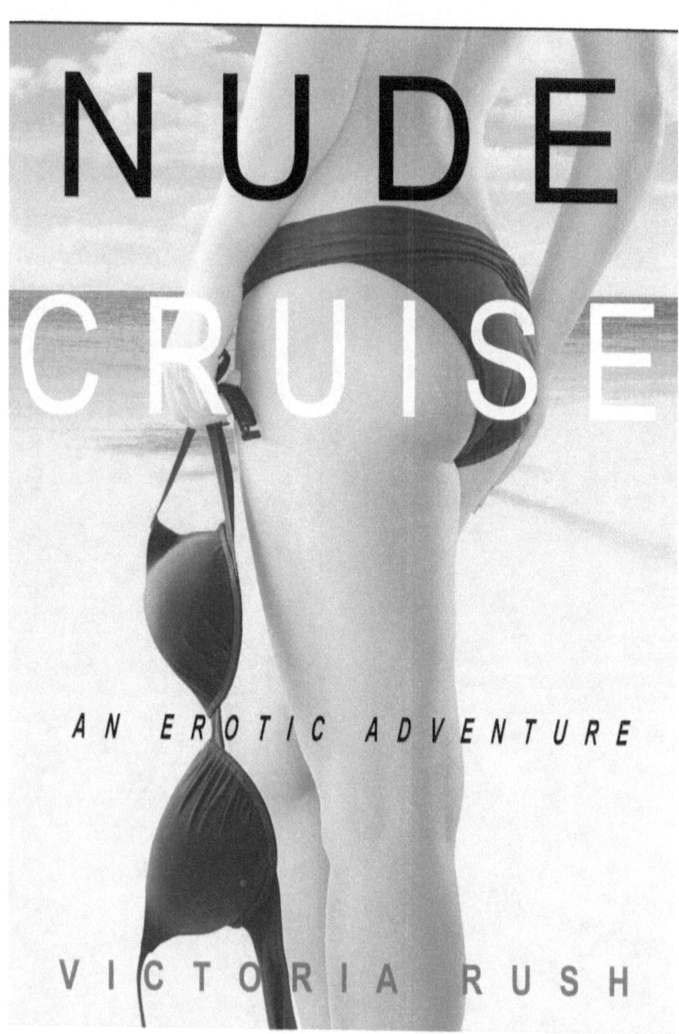

Some people get wet on a cruise for different reasons...

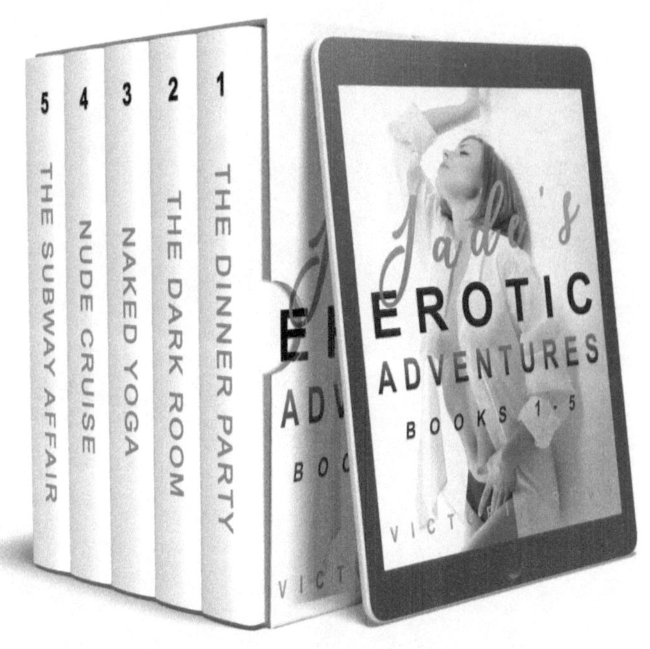

Books 1 -5 in the bestselling series - 60% off

THE DINNER PARTY - PREVIEW
FINGER FOOD

S ometime later, I heard a soft tap on my bedroom door. Not wanting to remove myself just yet from my cocoon of luxury, I called out to answer.

"Yes?"

"It's time for your massage," a woman's voice replied.

"Just one minute please."

I reluctantly stepped out of the bath and quickly toweled myself dry. I wrapped a large bath sheet around me, re-donned my mask, then opened the bedroom door.

A petite young Asian girl greeted me, wearing a kimono similar to mine and a crimson masquerade mask.

Apparently not everybody who works here always walks around stark naked.

The girl was utterly breathtaking. Long jet-black hair cascaded over high cheekbones past pouty lips, her delicate collarbones peeking from the top of her kimono. I could see her breasts and hips outlined by the tightly-wrapped kimono and suddenly wished that she too had come to my boudoir naked.

"My name is Jasmine," she said. "I'm your personal

masseuse and esthetician. Are you ready for your final preparation?

Just the thought of this beauty laying her tender hands on me sent a shiver down my spine.

"Definitely. Please come in. How would you like me to prepare?"

"Come with me, please."

Jasmine led me into the bathroom, where she nonchalantly removed her kimono and hung it behind the bathroom door.

Oh my God.

I didn't think anyone in this place could get more beautiful or sensuous. Jasmine had perfectly shaped B-cup breasts with a thin indentation running down the center of her perfectly toned stomach. Like everyone else in this place, her pubis was utterly bald and flawless. She barely looked eighteen and I was just about to ask her age, but she spoke first.

"If you'd like to remove your towel and lay face down on the table, we can get started. May I call you Jade?"

There was something about her confident manner and tone that belied her youthful appearance. I had no inhibitions whatsoever about displaying myself unclothed to this stranger.

"Yes, thank you, Jasmine." I unhooked my bath sheet and threw it against the side of the tub.

"Would you like me to drape your backside?" Jasmine asked.

"That won't be necessary," I quickly answered.

Jasmine walked over to the vanity counter and picked up two small bottles of oil resting under an orange radiant lamp. She brought them back to the massage table, opened one, and poured the oil into one cupped hand then rubbed her hands together. The scent of lavender wafted toward my nose.

I closed my eyes in anticipation of her touch. I'd had massages before, but nothing as sensuous and stimulating as this. When her hands touched the small of my back, I jerked reflexively from the sexual tension. My heart was beating a hundred miles an hour as I felt the blood coursing through my veins.

Jasmine must have sensed my nervous tension and began pressing her fingers more firmly into my back as she moved them slowly up each side of my spine. The warm oil allowed her hands to glide effortlessly across my skin. She used every surface of her hands to massage my muscles, expertly kneading my skin with her fingers and palm.

I began to relax as my muscles softened and surrendered to her touch. She sensuously massaged every part of my back, shoulders, and neck, applying just the right amount of pressure. Periodically, she would pour more warm oil on my lower back, dipping her hands in it to replenish the silky lubrication against my pliant skin.

Just as the sexual tension began to subside from the utter relaxation of the massage, Jasmine moved her hands down to my buttocks and began to caress them in soft circular motions. My glutes contracted involuntarily and I unconsciously pressed my mound into the firm padding of the table. Suddenly I was quickly reminded that a gorgeous young woman was caressing my naked body. She cupped each buttock between her hands as she massaged my ass tantalizingly, her little finger sliding slowly into the cleft just above my anus.

Periodically, I'd partially open one of my eyes with my head turned in her direction to look at her gorgeous body. My head was at the same level as her midsection, and my mouth watered as I watched her stomach muscles flex and her hips undulate with each movement of her hands. At times her pussy was almost right beside me and I wanted to reach out and run my own fingers up her soft legs.

I was in total heaven and getting wetter by the moment. Just when I thought I couldn't stand it anymore, she suddenly moved her hands down to my feet and began massaging her thumbs into my soles.

I'd always loved having my feet massaged, but nobody did it like Jasmine. She cradled my foot and used every part of her hands to massage and knead every surface from my heel to my toes. I didn't want her to stop, but there were other parts of my body that were screaming for attention.

As if reading my thoughts, she began moving her hands up toward my calf, using her thumbs to spread the muscle apart. She lingered almost as long on my calf as she had on my foot, rolling the ball of my calf between both of her hands, sliding her slick hands up and down erotically. I couldn't help imagining how she might use those same hands to massage a man's erect cock in a similar manner. My mind wandered again to what pleasures lay in wait for me over dinner.

After shifting her hands to my right leg and giving my other foot and calf similar attention, she placed each hand just behind my knees and began to slowly move them up towards my buttocks. Her thumbs pressed against my inner thighs as she glided tantalizingly close to my apex.

I rolled my legs outward in an invitation to move closer. My legs were parted enough that I was sure she could see my vulva from her vantage point behind me. In my highly aroused state, my lips were engorged and spread apart, revealing my moist and quivering opening.

But as much as I desperately wanted her to, Jasmine

never touched me there. She repeatedly slid her hands right up to the edge of my slit, pressing and rotating her thumbs on the fleshy meat of my upper thighs just below my aching pussy. I suppose this was part of her master plan—to tease me mercilessly and inflame my passions so I'd be ready for just about anything at the main event.

It was certainly working. After thirty minutes of Jasmine's ministrations, I was grinding my pussy into the table trying desperately to give my clit some needed direct stimulation.

Just when I thought I couldn't be teased any more tantalizingly, Jasmine opened one of the bottles of warm oil and poured it directly into the crack of my ass. She paused as the fluid flowed down and directly over my parted lips. I almost came from the gentle movement of the warm liquid as it trickled across the folds of my labia, channeled toward the junction where they joined together at my clit. I shuddered in pleasure at the feeling, even if it was only the subtlest of touch.

Jasmine suddenly interrupted my thoughts.

"Would you like to turn over now?"

It was the first time she had spoken directly to me since the massage started, and it surprised me in my catatonic, pre-orgasmic state. I practically flipped over like a fish out of water and spread my legs expectantly. Finally, I'd get some relief. Surely, she couldn't leave me hanging like this.

"It's time for your final grooming," she said. "I'll need you to part your legs a bit further to provide full access."

Grooming? I knew this was part of the process, but somehow it didn't seem fair to transition at this precise moment. At least I'd be able to stay on the comfortable massage table instead of the clinical vinyl chairs used by my regular esthetician.

Jasmine walked over to another cabinet by the makeup table and withdrew a leather bag from one of the drawers, then brought it back to the table. She reached into the bag and pulled out a cordless hair trimmer.

"Do you have a preference regarding your appearance?" she asked. "Do you prefer natural, neatly trimmed, or bare?"

I knew she was referring to my pubic hair, which I generally kept neatly trimmed. I'd always thought going fully bald was unnatural and unseemly, catering to men's prurient fantasies of fucking young schoolgirls. But in this situation, it seemed entirely appropriate, like I was stripping away all my camouflage and armor.

If tonight was all about being watched, I might as well bare myself in every sense of the word and truly let my inhibitions go. I began to fantasize about rubbing my bare pussy against Jasmine's while she poured warm oil between us. The more work she had to do on me, the more chance I'd have to make this last and hopefully get off.

I didn't hesitate. "Bare, thank you."

"As you wish," she said. "I'll remove the long hairs first with the trimmer, then shave you smooth with a razor."

No waxing? This was different. I was relieved to not have to bear the painful and violent trial of having my hairs ripped out en masse. Although shaving down there was always a scary proposition, I felt safe in the capable and practiced hands of this beautiful esthetician.

Jasmine nodded, then flipped a switch on the trimmer. The device buzzed softly as she placed it gently on my mound. I had only a light dusting of fur and it didn't take long for her to remove it with a few short strokes over my pubis. I shuddered as the vibrations penetrated deep into my core. If she had placed the flat head on my clitoris, I would have popped off in a millisecond. Instead, she turned the trimmer face-down and gently swiped the vibrating teeth against the sides of my vulva, sensuously separating my labia with her hands as she moved the device between my legs to trim the hairs on the inside and outside of my labia.

It was an insanely titillating feeling, but just clinical enough to bring me down from my plateau and shift my focus. My mind wandered to the upcoming feast, and I contemplated what surprises lay in wait at the main event. The hostesses had suggested there would be 'contact' of some sort during the meal, and I was intrigued exactly who and how it would be administered. The idea of being fully bald, cleansed, and thoroughly stimulated going into the event was an incredible rush.

Jasmine continued with the trimmer all the way down my perineum to my anus, barely touching me with the trimmer so as not to pinch any delicate tissues. Apparently there were no parts of my erogenous zone that would remain untouched, now—and perhaps later.

She turned off the trimmer and placed it at the foot of the table. Then she took a bottle of gel from the bag and spread the gel on her hands. Using both hands, she spread it gently between my legs, starting on my mound all the way down to my rosebud.

My body almost levitated above the table as Jasmine finally laid her hands directly on my clitoris. The gel had a mild stinging quality that added to the stimulating sensation. If this was meant to excite my follicles in preparation for the shave, it wasn't the only feature of my anatomy that it made erect. I could feel the hood of my clitoris retract as my button filled with blood and began to push outward. Suddenly, I was fully stimulated again and lusting for Jasmine's touch. I fantasized about her bending down and taking my swollen nub between her puffy lips and letting me come in her mouth.

Unfortunately, my satisfaction would have to wait a little longer. Instead, Jasmine reached into her bag and pulled out a straight-edge razor. In anyone else's hands, it might look threatening, especially in my prostrated and vulnerable position. But something about the way she delicately and sensuously opened the jackknifed tool instantly evaporated my fears. I could see how this type of razor would in fact give her better control safely cutting my stubs instead of the usual ladies plastic razor.

With her right hand, Jasmine gently laid the razor on its flat edge at the top of my mound, while she gently pulled my skin upwards with her other hand. Then she slowly turned the sharp edge perpendicular to my skin and began softly scraping the razor downwards. I could hear the bristling sound as the razor edge removed my nubs right down to the follicles. She repeated the pattern in one inch wide swipes on one side then the other of my pubis, being ever-so-careful to stop just where my clitoris lay quivering in a mixture of fear and excitement. There was something about the utter vulnerability of the procedure that made it the most erotic experience I'd ever had.

Jasmine used the same deft touch as she moved down my vulva and perineum, scraping the vestiges of stray hairs away with gentle swipes of the long blade, while sensuously separating my folds and flesh with her other hand. She took extra time and care around my anus and clit, using the gentlest and slowest motion I've ever felt someone apply to my body. The combination of fright and titillation as she probed my most sensitive body parts created a river of sensuous fluids running down my vulva. By this time, no shaving gel was necessary to provide a smooth gliding surface for the knife.

When she was finished, Jasmine retrieved a fresh wash towel from beside the sink and held it under the warm water faucet then twisted the excess water into the basin. She returned to the table and placed it over my splayed legs then gently cleansed the excess moisture and remaining shaving gel with gentle massaging movements of her hands. The warm, moist towel felt exquisite against my newly shaved skin. Jasmine's hands now felt comforting between my legs rather than erotic.

She had taken me on an incredibly sensuous erotic arc, right to the edge of ecstasy and back, to a quiet relaxed place. I exhaled fully and completely for the first time in almost an hour.

Jasmine removed the towel from between my legs and held up a large hand mirror at a forty-five degree angle toward me.

"What do you think?" she asked.

I tilted my head up and studied her masterpiece. Far from the usual red and swollen vulva that I typically experienced after the violent waxing with my regular esthetician, I'd never seen my pussy look so beautiful. Utterly bereft of any hair, my entire perineum from my pubic mound to my anus was totally bald, pink—and gorgeous. I just stared at my beautiful pussy, utterly transfixed by the transformation.

"You have to *feel* it to really appreciate how beautiful you are, Jade," Jasmine purred.

I moved my right hand down, running my fingers along the edges of my pussy. I gasped from a feeling I'd never felt before. It felt smooth as silk: no bumps or blemishes or cuts or bruises. It was almost as if I was feeling somebody else— somebody I'd never felt before. I couldn't stop my left hand joining the other in rubbing and caressing my sensitive organs.

Jasmine lowered the mirror and smiled at me as I felt the moisture begin to accumulate between my legs again.

"It's almost time for your dinner appointment," she said. "Why don't you save the best for last? I think you'll find plenty of ways to satisfy your appetite over the next couple of hours."

She lifted my kimono from the hook at the edge of the bathtub and held it open for me.

"I'll escort you downstairs now if you're ready. All you need to bring is your kimono and slippers—and your mask of course."

I sat up slowly and stepped off the massage table. Turning around, I held my arms out as Jasmine lifted one arm of the silk robe onto me then the other. Then she turned around to face me, wrapped the silk tie around me, and tied a single bow over my belly button. She retrieved my matching silk slippers and knelt down on one knee to gently lift my feet one at a time and place them softly inside. It took every ounce of my power not to grab her head and pull it into my pulsating pussy.

Jasmine stood up gracefully and smiled into my eyes.

"If you'll follow me, I'll escort you now to the fantasy feast."

She didn't bother putting her own robe on. Her tight little ass barely jiggled as she stepped smartly ahead of me. I wasn't sure if I'd have a chance to feel Jasmine's touch again before the evening was over, but for now I was in total bliss ogling her petite, curvaceous figure from behind...

Read More

ABOUT THE AUTHOR

If you would like to receive notification of new book(s) in Jade's Erotic Adventures, follow me at http://bookbub.com/authors/victoria-rush.

If you have a moment, please post a brief review on my Amazon book page at view book.at/sse . Even just a couple of sentences will help other readers find and enjoy this book as much as you hopefully did.

Follow, share, like, and comment at:

www.facebook.com/authorvictoriarush
www.pinterest.com/authorvictoriarush
www.twitter.com/authorvictoriarush
authorvictoriarush@outlook.com

Hope to see you again soon!

www.ingramcontent.com/pod-product-compliance
Lightning Source LLC
Chambersburg PA
CBHW030822200726
48288CB00004B/1346